Going Places

ON A PLANE

By Robert M. Hamilton

Gareth Stevens
Publishing

Please visit our website, www.garethstevens.com. For a free color catalog of all our high-quality books, call toll free 1-800-542-2595 or fax 1-877-542-2596.

Library of Congress Cataloging-in-Publication Data

Hamilton, Robert M., 1987-
On a plane / Robert M. Hamilton.
    p. cm. — (Going places)
Includes index.
ISBN 978-1-4339-6279-0 (pbk.)
ISBN 978-1-4339-6280-6 (6-pack)
ISBN 978-1-4339-6277-6 (library binding)
1. Airplanes—Juvenile literature. 2. Air travel—Juvenile literature. I. Title.
TL547.H1476 2012
387.7'42—dc23

2011031219

First Edition

Published in 2012 by
Gareth Stevens Publishing
111 East 14th Street, Suite 349
New York, NY 10003

Copyright © 2012 Gareth Stevens Publishing

Editor: Katie Kawa
Designer: Andrea Davison-Bartolotta

Photo credits: Cover, pp. 7, 9, 11, 15, 17, 19, 21, 23, 24 (cockpit, wings) Shutterstock.com; p. 1 Jupiterimages/Creatas/Thinkstock; p. 5 Hemera/Thinkstock; pp. 13, 24 (pilot) Ryan McVay/Photodisc/Thinkstock.

Printed in the United States of America

CPSIA compliance information: Batch #CW12GS: For further information contact Gareth Stevens, New York, New York at 1-800-542-2595.

Contents

Planes can fly.

First, they move
on wheels.

They move fast
on the ground.
Then, they start to fly.

They have wings.
Wings keep them
in the air.

One person flies a plane. He is the pilot.

He sits in the front
of the plane.
This place is called
the cockpit.

One kind of plane
is a seaplane.
It can land on water.

Another kind is
a biplane.
It has two wings.

The first plane was
a biplane.

21

It was made more than 100 years ago!

23

Words to Know

cockpit

pilot

wings

Index